PEEKABOO POO!

Written by Lisa Regan

Illustrated by Richard Watson

BONNEY PRESS

For Maya and Jae

P.S.

Published by Bonney Press
an imprint of Hinkler Books Pty Ltd
45–55 Fairchild Street
Heatherton Victoria 3202 Australia
www.hinkler.com

BONNEY
PRESS

Author: Lisa Regan
Illustrator: Richard Watson
Editorial: Emily Murray
Art Director: Paul Scott

ISBN: 978 1 4889 1049 4

Printed and bound in China

PEEKABOO POO!

Alfie has a present for you...

Alfie is a little scamp. He can walk and burp and laugh.
He loves choo choo trains and pets and blowing bubbles in the bath.

Alf still wears a nappy, because he's only two.

He doesn't need to worry about
where he does a poo!

Then Mummy speaks to Alfie.
She says, 'I think that you're ready,

To start using the potty now.

It's simple – just watch teddy!'

Mummy pulls Alf's nappy down and seats him with a grin.
The potty feels too big at first,
he's scared he might fall in!

'You've got it!'
squeals his mummy. 'So, that's what you should do,
If you're playing and you feel the urge, sit there to do a poo.'

Alfie doesn't need to poo, but a bit of wee comes out.

It won't stay in the potty though,

it's squirting all about!

Mummy smiles and gets a cloth, and gives him a big cuddle.
'Don't worry if you miss at first, we'll soon wipe up the puddle.'

Then Mummy leaves him to it, and Alfie starts to play.
He soon forgets the poos and wees and gets on with his day.

The train is going round the track as Alfie shouts, 'Choo choo!'
And then he feels his tummy squeeze and
knows he needs to poo.

Alfie wants his nappy back.
This potty thing's no fun!

He thinks there must be other places where **pooing can be done.**

He tries to find his potty, but then comes up with a plan.

Who needs a boring potty when

he could use...this pan!

Alfie sits as he was shown. The pan is very cold!

He thinks his plan is genius

for someone two years old.

Mum walks in the kitchen; her nose detects a stink.

Little Alf has left the pooey pan...

...beneath the kitchen sink.

Alfie feels quite happy. He's started a new game.

And so begins his master plan:
the peek-a-poo campaign!

Daddy needs to go to work. He kisses them goodbye.

He checks his hair, puts on his coat, and straightens up his tie.

And then he settles on the stair to fasten up his shoe.

Oops! That's when he finds the next place where Alfie's done a poo!

Buster's in the garden.

He's digging in the ground.

He pants and barks quite happily.

Look what he has found!

He goes into his kennel to chew it on his mat.

But as he steps inside the door, something brown **goes splat!**

Brother Charlie's home from school. He's going to play a game.

He plays online for ages, and his friends all do the same.

Charlie turns the TV on then settles in his chair.

Disaster strikes!

Too late, he finds that Alfie's poo is there!

Mummy's gone out
for the day
and Grandma's
here to help.

She goes into the
bathroom and
Alfie hears a yelp.

Poor Grandma sorts the laundry, and naughty Alfie knows
she's found the poo he did last night,
hidden in the clothes.

Grandpa's in the garden, pulling out the weeds.

He wants to get it tidy so that he can plant some seeds.

He potters in
the garden shed.
But what's that
funny smell?

Alfie's still not
toilet trained,
but a pot works
just as well!

Sister Kate is going out. Getting ready takes her hours.

No one else can use the loo while she preens, primps and showers.

She steps into the bathtub and reaches for the tap.

'That's gross!' she shrieks.
'Disgusting! Poo in my shower cap!'

Mummy knows it's time to chat. She sits Alf on her knee.

'PLEASE try to use your potty, Alf, when you poo and wee.'

'You seem to think it's funny, hiding poos in all our stuff,

But sweetie it's our family home, and now we've had enough.'

Alfie wriggles off her knee, a smile upon his face.
He shows his mummy proudly –

a poo in the right place!